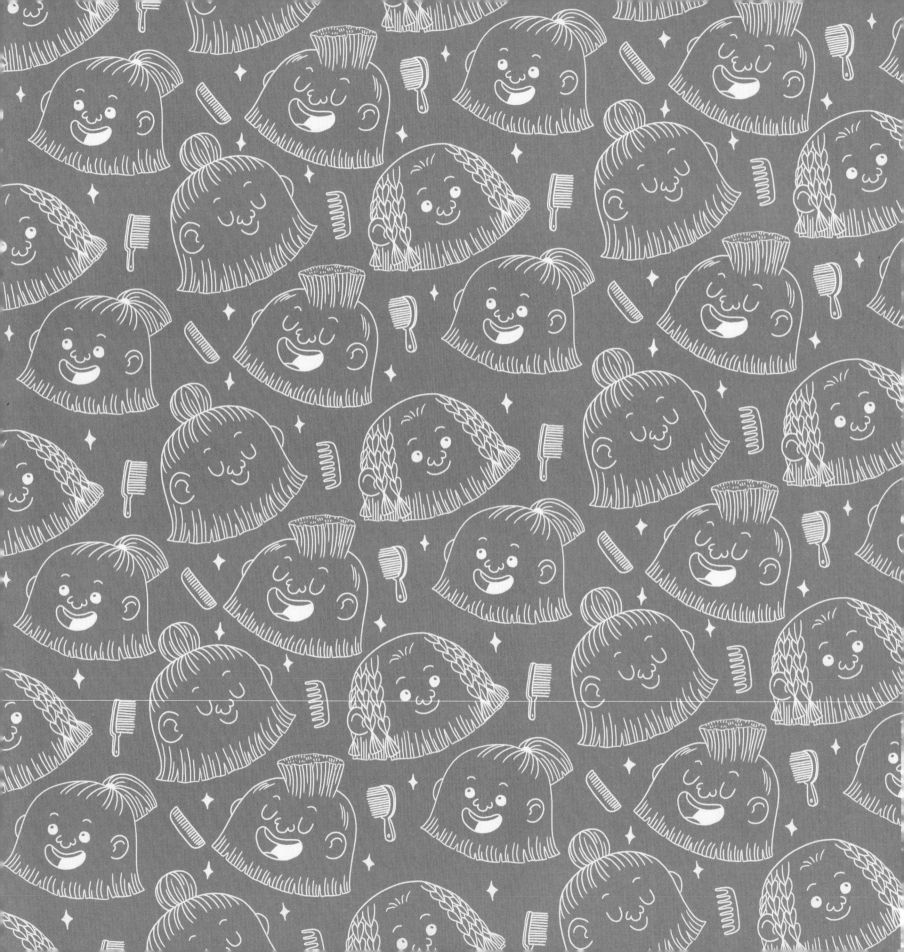

I LOVE MY FUR!

KELLY LEIGH MILLER

FOR HOPE & MELISSA, WHO HAVE AMAZING HAIR

SIMON & SCHUSTER BOOKS FOR YOUNG READERS
An imprint of Simon & Schuster Children's Publishing Division
1230 Avenue of the Americas, New York, New York 10020
© 2021 by Kelly Leigh Miller
Book design by Lucy Ruth Cummins © 2021 by Simon & Schuster, Inc.
SIMON & SCHUSTER BOOKS FOR YOUNG READERS and related marks are
trademarks of Simon & Schuster, Inc.
For information about special discounts for bulk purchases, please contact
Simon & Schuster Special Sales at 1-866-506-1949 or business@simonandschuster.com.
The Simon & Schuster Speakers Bureau can bring authors to your live event. For more information
or to book an event, contact the Simon & Schuster Speakers Bureau at 1-866-248-3049 or visit our
website at www.simonspeakers.com.
The text for this book was hand-lettered.
The illustrations for this book were rendered digitally.
Manufactured in China
0221 SCP
First Edition
2 4 6 8 10 9 7 5 3 1
Library of Congress Cataloging-in-Publication Data
Names: Miller, Kelly Leigh, author, illustrator.
Title: I love my fur! / Kelly Leigh Miller.
Description: First edition. | New York : Simon & Schuster Books for Young Readers, [2021] |
Audience: Ages 4–8. | Audience: Grades K–1. | Summary: Bigfoot loves his soft, shiny fur so much it
begins to affect his relationships with his friends.
Identifiers: LCCN 2020025271 | ISBN 9781534478954 (hardcover) | ISBN 9781534478961 (ebook)
Subjects: CYAC: Sasquatch—Fiction. | Hair—Fiction.
Classification: LCC PZ7.1.M5815 Ias 2021 | DDC [E]—dc23
LC record available at https://lccn.loc.gov/2020025271

I LOVE MY FUR!

KELLY LEIGH MILLER

SIMON & SCHUSTER BOOKS FOR YOUNG READERS
New York London Toronto Sydney New Delhi

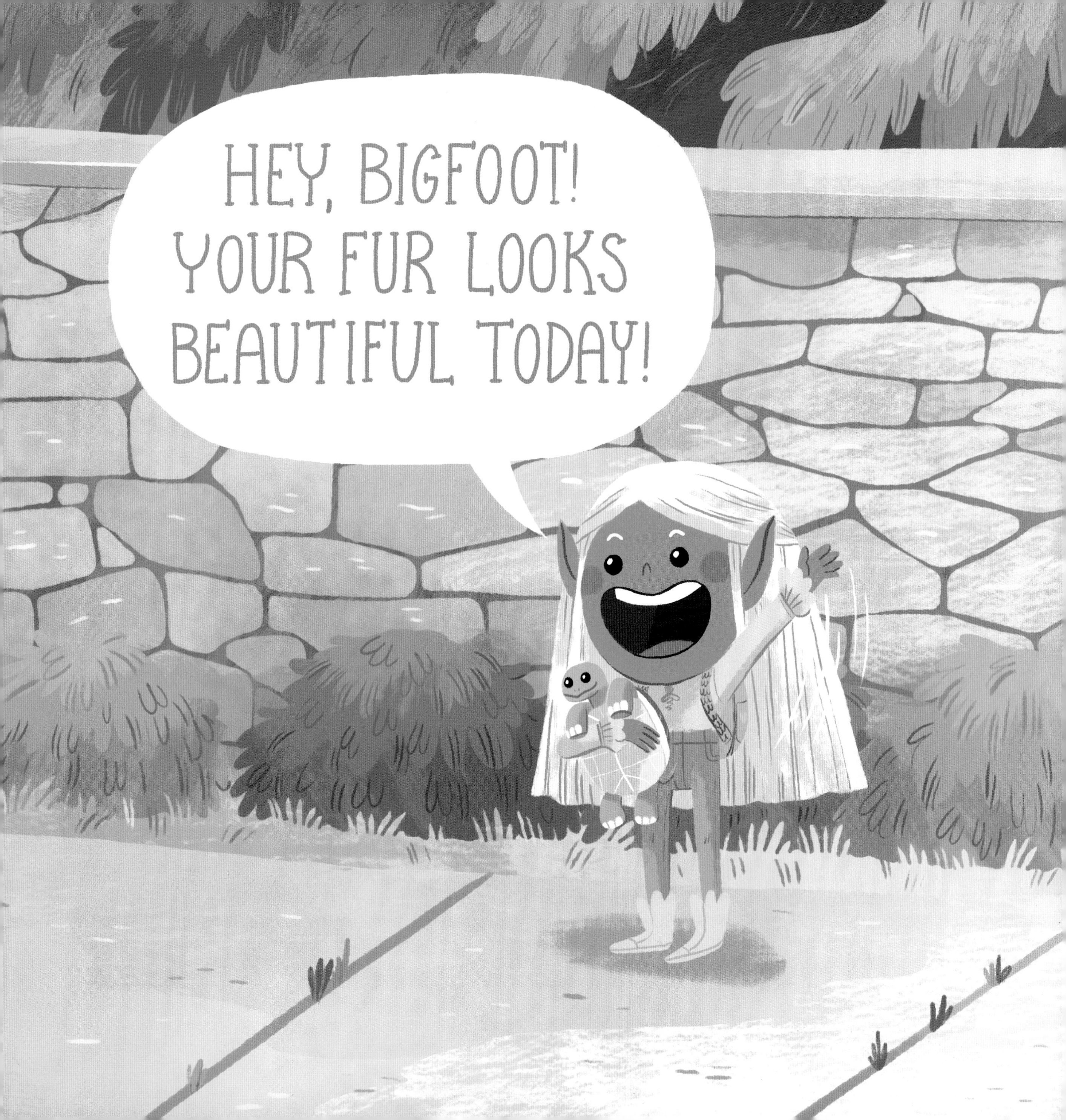
HEY, BIGFOOT! YOUR FUR LOOKS BEAUTIFUL TODAY!

I LOVE MY FUR!
IT'S SO FLUFFY!
IT'S SO SOFT!

IT'S THE MOST BEAUTIFUL
FUR ANYONE'S EVER SEEN!

IT'S ALL ANYONE WANTS
TO TALK ABOUT.

HAVE YOU SEEN MY
NEW BOOK?

I TRY MY BEST TO HELP OTHERS.

MAYBE, IF YOU BRUSH YOUR FUR EVERY DAY, IT WILL LOOK LIKE MINE!

SLAM!

YOU SHOULD WEAR YOUR HAIR DOWN THE WAY I DO!

IF YOU CONDITION IT, YOUR HAIR WILL BE AS SOFT AS MINE!
I DON'T HAVE HAIR.
MY HAIR IS SNAKES.

BIGFOOT, I THINK IT'S TIME FOR A FURCUT.
MOTHER, FUR THIS BEAUTIFUL SHOULD NEVER BE CUT.

NEVER...

EVER...

SHOW-AND-TELL

YES,

LOVES

MY

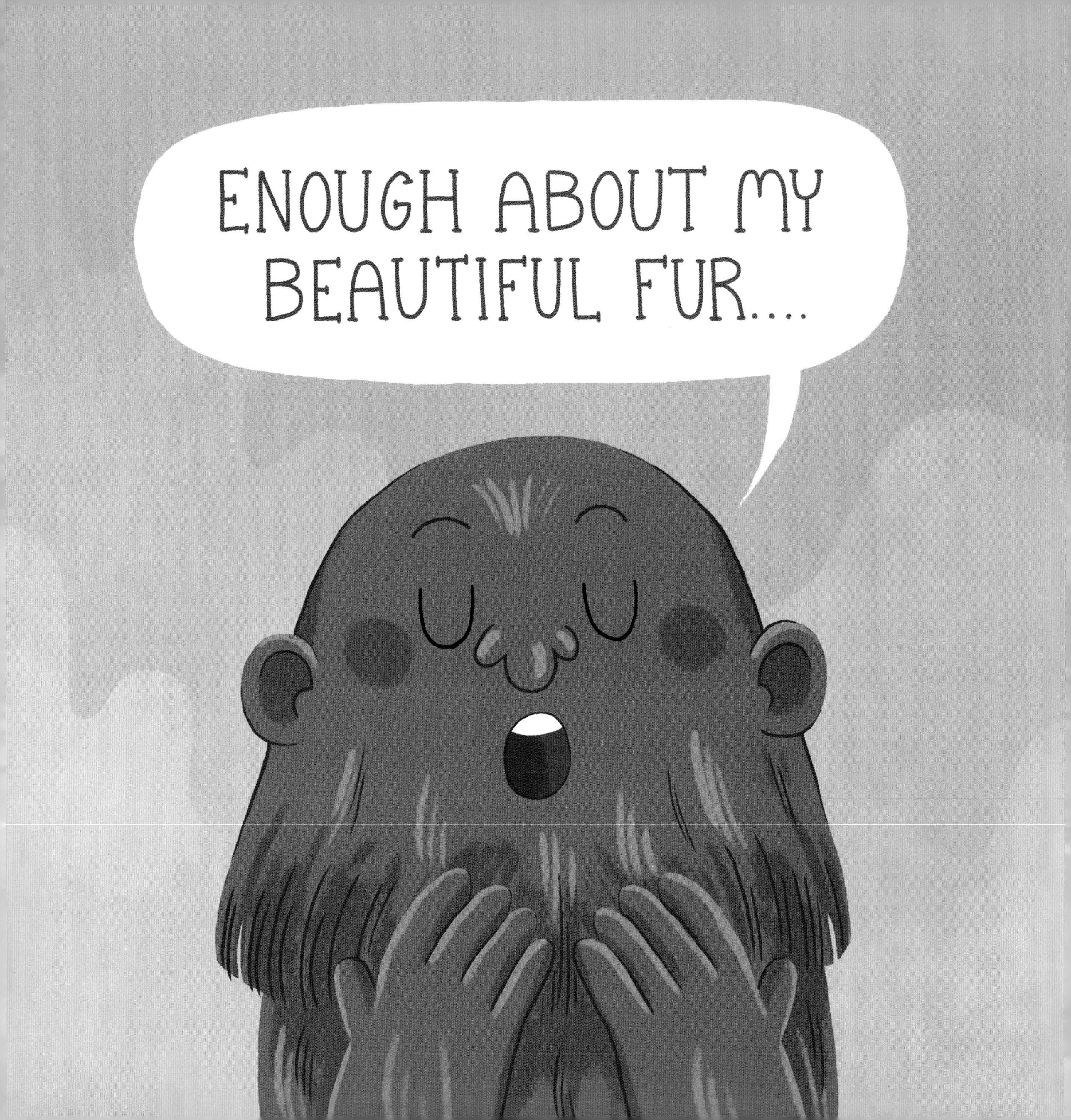
ENOUGH ABOUT MY BEAUTIFUL FUR....

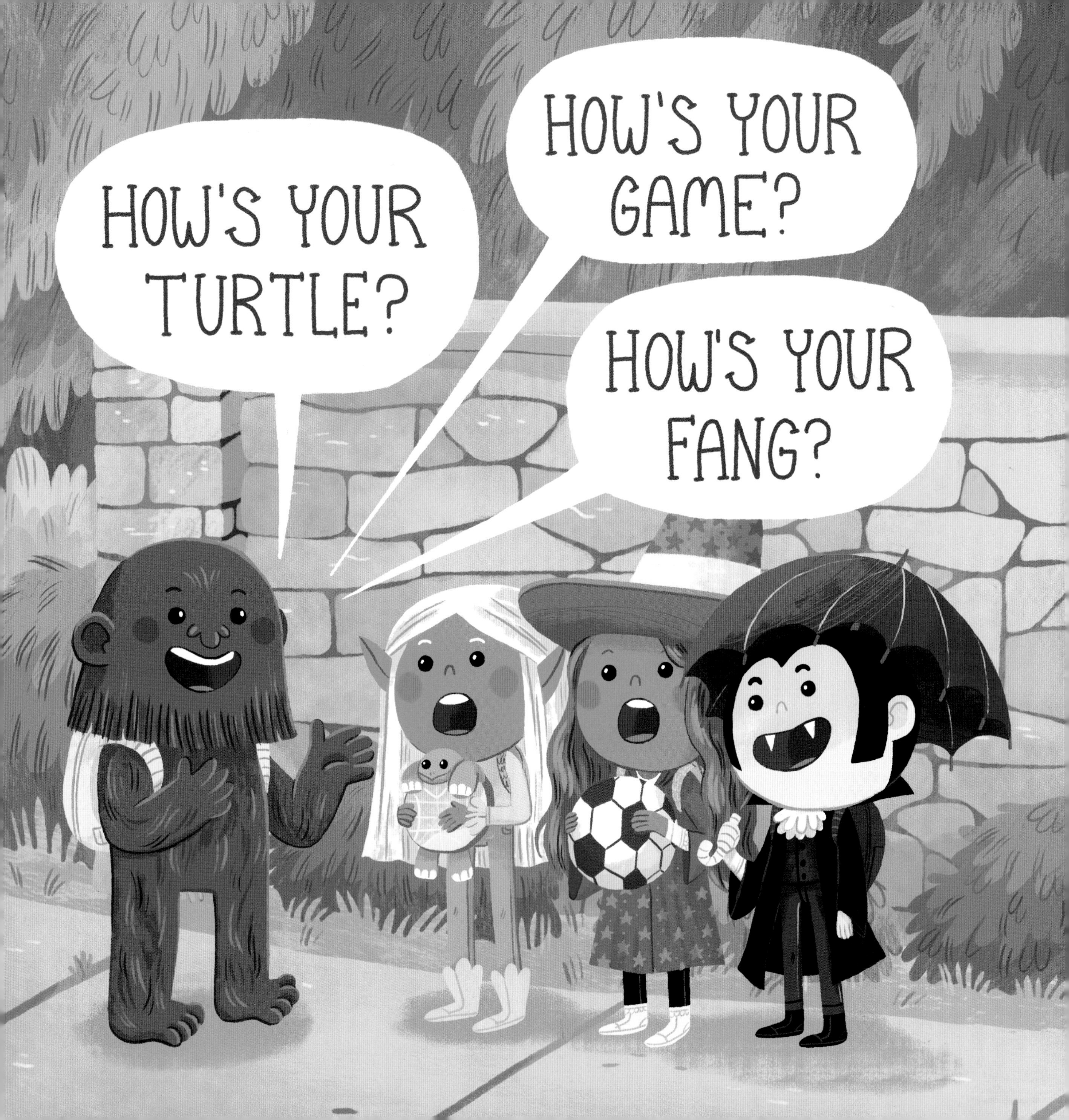
HOW'S YOUR TURTLE?
HOW'S YOUR GAME?
HOW'S YOUR FANG?

I STILL LOVE MY FUR.

IT'S SO SHINY.

IT'S SO SOFT.

BUT...

I ALSO LOVE WHAT MY FRIENDS LIKE TO DO!

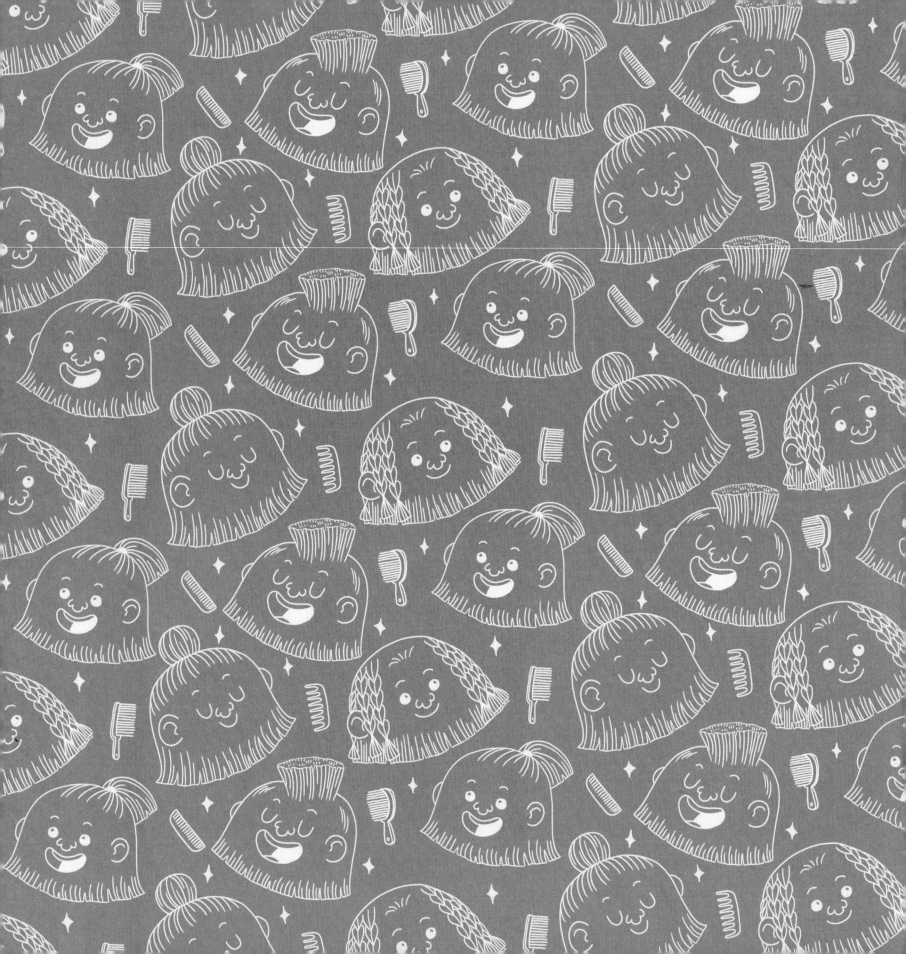